CHEE

RISING

LEGACY

SABAH'S STORY
PART 1

GW00863394

Written and Illustrated

by

HANNAH E. ENGLAND

ISBN-13: 979-8-3620-6276-7

PRONUNCIATION GUIDE

SABAH: sah-bah

RAIDEN: ray-din

RAKIM: rah-keem

FUMNAYA: foom-nah-yah

RAISA: rye-ee-sah

JAMAA: jah-mah

ELIM: ee-lim

CHIMA: chee-mah

TABLE OF CONTENTS

CHAPTER ONE

SABAH

A spotted streamline cat made her way across the African plains at a quick trot. Her ears twitched at every other sound made in the endless tall grass before her. One could never be too careful, and she of all animals knew it very well. She was a cheetah, a very fast but often nervous kind of animal, and all for good reasons. There were many strong predators on the Serengeti that could easily make an end of her, and they wouldn't show her any mercy if she was caught. This should have made her a bit more cautious, but she had an adventurous, fiery personality since cubhood. It had never left, but only became more cunning and subtle as she aged. Her name was Sabah.

Growing up, she had been one of six

cubs. Two of them didn't make it to adulthood, but the others had fought valiantly for their lives and conquered the odds. She had shared many adventures with them, but they were gone now. She had grown up, and that meant living alone, until she had her own cubs.

The young cheetah brothers and sisters had split up nearly a month ago, and Sabah had become used to being alone; in fact she liked it immensely. She remembered her siblings so vividly. Sometimes it seemed they were standing in front of her. Raiden, with his careful, intelligent eyes, Rakim, his rough and slightly reckless personality, much like her own, and of course dear Fumnaya, pretty, sometimes timid, but strong. *Oh Fumnaya*, Sabah thought as she continued trotting along the plains, *if only we could have been together those last days without fighting.* With them gone, Sabah wasn't upset at all. They had been wonderful siblings, but times were different. *I hope they all are doing well,* she thought.

Sabah paused and listened. In the distance she could hear the thundering sounds of lions announcing their ownership of the very land she stood on. She listened as the voices continued to rise and fall, and wondered how much louder they would be if they were close by. Their voices were so powerful, they could be heard miles away from where she stood. Sabah was glad they were roaring. She wasn't interested in getting torn to pieces, and it helped her to have a sense of where they were.

I suppose they have to warn other lions that they live here, she thought, *but why alert the prey in the area as well? I'm trying to hunt, blast them!* She knew gazelles and impala would be on high alert after hearing all that, as would she.

Sabah continued on her way, keeping a low profile. She did not hunt successfully that day, and as night approached, a frustrated growl escaped her. She hated going to sleep hungry, even though she did very often. She settled down to sleep on a high rock. There were too many dangers like lions, leopards, and hyenas for her to be out and exposed.

At the break of dawn, she was on the

move again, her stomach aching for meat, her mind, sharp and clear. As she made her way through the plains, the Serengeti became lively. There was a herd of elephants to her right that rumbled at her as she walked, and to her left, a herd of zebras snorted at her as she slunk past.

Sabah didn't like that. She needed to surprise her prey if she was going to eat; their alarm could cost her. She suddenly stiffened. The wind had brought her the smell of a carcass not a long way off, but that was not what had made her freeze; the wind also carried the scent of hyenas.

The zebras snorted and wheeled, for they too had caught the unmistakable scent. Their hooves pounded the ground as they gathered together, and with laid back ears, they glared at the cheetah as she glided by.

Sabah crouched instinctively, showing her teeth, and hissed softly. She raised her head over the grass and realized she could actually see the hyenas gathered around their kill in the distance. Sabah knew as long as they had a kill and were actively feeding on it, that was most likely where they would stay. She decided to slink past them, but to try and stay out of sight.

As she neared the hyenas, she could hear the chaos of the feeding. The snapping of jaws and cracking of bones, along with the shrieks from the hyenas, made her blood curdle. She was glad when she made it past, and once again she turned her mind to hunting.

At last! She could see a herd of impala clustered around shrubbery. Sheltered from the sun and tucked away from the hyenas, they appeared undisturbed. Sabah lowered her head, and her eyes focused on them; her body became still. She slowly lifted a paw and began to stalk. Gently moving and halting, she inched her way closer and selected her target. She sucked in a breath of air, and then charged.

Like a coiled serpent, she struck at her prey, but quicker still, her prey leaped away from her, alerting each other with their bounding bodies and alarm calls. Sabah hadn't lost her target, and streaked after the impala.

The impala of her choice made a high bound that nearly made her vanish from the cheetah's sight, but as the animal came back down to earth, Sabah stretched out a paw and managed to hook a back leg. She quickly slapped the impala with her other paw, brought her down, and finished with a swift bite to the neck.

Crouched over her prize, she panted hard. The chase had lasted for hardly a minute, but she was drained. She had begun to feel weak from hunger, and the growing heat didn't help. It was a well earned meal for her. If she had been able to count or clock her own run, she would have known she had nearly exceeded fifty miles an hour during her chase.

She had run the impala out of the trees and bushes where they had clustered, and already vultures were gathering overhead, and slowly floating down to earth. *They never miss a meal do they?* thought Sabah, still too tired to eat. She wondered if it had been worthwhile to hunt with hyenas close by. After all, the gathering of the vultures would be sure to make them investigate the cause whether they were hungry or not.

After regaining her breath, Sabah tore into her meal, wolfing down the meat as fast as possible. The number of vultures increased dramatically, and made her more wary. Feeling crowded, she growled at them. Although they could try to push her off her kill, she was more worried about the attention they could attract.

She finally decided enough was enough. With her stomach full, there was no need to stick around. She walked away feeling quite relieved to do so as a jackal appeared nervously behind her, hoping for a bite. He flicked his eyes nervously in her direction, but she ignored him and continued on her way.

CHAPTER TWO

A YEARNING

Sabah found a termite mound in her wandering and climbed on top. There she perched, just like her mother used to do when she was little, but Sabah was not thinking about Raisa. Instead, she was scanning the plains for any animal that could possibly concern her. Satisfied she was safe at the moment, she curled down, her head resting lightly on one shoulder, and waited for her food to digest.

This was the life of a cheetah - hunt, rest, look out for danger, sleep, and look out for danger again. It was an exhausting way to live, but Sabah didn't know any different. Her agility always carried her to safety in the nick of time. There was also her independent personality to contend with; it always pushed her to take risks, all in the name of survival.

Fortunately for her, over time she would calm down, as there was nothing for her to prove. She had already done that by making it so far and continuing to thrive. As a female cheetah, she was always wandering, exploring, resting, hunting, and exploring again, and she loved it.

Some days later, Sabah began to feel a deep yearning inside of her. It was unlike anything she had ever felt before. She yearned for someone to nurture, to talk to, and to defend. It was a feeling much bigger than her, and she was well aware of that. Up until this point she had been happy alone, but there was no questioning this feeling. *This was how my mother felt before she had us,* Sabah thought to herself one day. *There's just no mistaking this. I want cubs.*

She was surprised that she felt this way so soon, but after thinking about it for a moment, she realized it was everything she had ever wanted, though not in the way her past self had thought. What better way to satisfy her need to prove to the world her strength and independence, than to rear cubs to adulthood? And not just one or two, but *all* of them. Once the thought entered her head, there was no going back. Her mind was made up, her determination unbreakable.

If Raisa had been there and could have read her daughters thoughts, Sabah would have received a severe scolding. For Sabah to think that an inexperienced cheetah mother could raise a litter of cubs all on her own, without losing at least one, was mostly unheard of.

Sabah was young and ambitious, but did not entirely lack understanding. After sifting through her memories of cubhood and remembering the dangers she and her siblings faced, she began to wonder if she really *could* raise all her cubs as a first time mother. *It would take a miracle I suppose,* she thought sadly, *but there's no harm in trying. If I could beat the odds, so can they.*

Her determination was so great, she felt as though a lion would run at the sight of her. Her confidence swelled until she felt as though it would spill out of her ears, but the sound of more roars rolling in from miles away quickly shattered her fantasy. She shook herself, remembering she was just a slender cheetah and not a threat to any lion, but her determination remained.

Sabah realized that her new goal had changed her. She rose from where she had been laying in the shade. She was too restless to remain in the same place. The only thing she wanted was to begin her mission of raising cubs.

Not long after her yearning began, Sabah began to have flashes of forgotten memories of Raisa. It was as if her mind was preparing her for motherhood through vivid memories, or rather now that motherhood was near, she suddenly had more respect for her mother and what she had accomplished.

Looking back, she remembered that Raisa had mentioned a few times that they were not her first cubs. *How many litters did she go through until she was successful?* Sabah wondered. *She never really spoke much about any of her other cubs to us, but then again, maybe that was too strange for her.* There was one memory in particular that stood out to her, and as she lay stretched out on a termite mound, she briefly seemed to drift away into events long past.

"Mother!" Sabah cried, "what's that?"

Raisa lifted her head from nuzzling Faraji and looked questioningly at her daughter. "What are you looking at Sabah?" she asked, quickly sitting up. Her cubs chirped and tumbled off her, some rolling down the termite mound flailing their little paws.

"That!" Sabah pointed with her nose at a four legged figure coming their way.

Raisa took one look in the direction Sabah was pointing. She jumped to her feet and sprinted down the termite mound emitting loud chirp like cries of defiance. The cubs looked after her curiously, only to see her skillfully evade the jaws of death as a hyena snapped at her. The hyena let out a wild shriek of fury as he missed the spotted feline.

The cubs were frightened of that gaping mouth full of teeth and its sinister cry. They dashed into the grass, terrified and alone as their mother taunted the hyena with growls and half charges to allow the cubs time to escape. After a few moments, the cubs were lost in the tall grass, and there was nothing to be gained for the hyena from continuing to harass the enraged mother cheetah. With a final rush at her, he gave up and turned his back, his tail still fluffed to show he left only of his own accord, and had not been driven away.

Raisa watched him go, her head low, her teeth still bared and her tail between her legs. When he had vanished from sight, she turned and trotted towards the termite mound anxiously calling the cubs. There was no answer.

Sabah snapped back into reality. She quickly checked the surrounding area and heaved a sigh of relief. She had no idea why her mind kept returning to that memory. Perhaps it was the selfless bravery her mother showed in such a moment of danger.

She growled, irritated. Was this really the time to be haunted by memories of narrow escapes from her cubhood? She got up and stretched. This was certainly not the time to be thinking of old memories. It was time to hunt.

CHAPTER THREE

NEW ARRIVALS

As Sabah was bombarded by more and more memories of her mother's bravery, she answered the deep yearning inside of her to have cubs. Time passed, and she found herself nosing about more in the grass in preparation for the cub's arrival. She felt more serious about it than anything, not terribly excited like she had thought she would. Her memories had sobered her, for motherhood was at hand.

She needed to find a safe place for a den, and the soon to be mother cheetah now found herself feeling heavier by the day. Hunting became more of a struggle, until she found herself weaker and doing more scavenging than she was accustomed to. Finally, there came the day that brought the change she had so yearned for.

The sun had risen, delivering its blessed rays of hope to the animals that were forced to huddle together during the terrors of the night. The light found Sabah nestled deeply in a shaded area full of bushes and tall grass. Snuggled against her were three little cubs. They had light grey fur covering their backs, with soft defenseless bodies capable only of tiny wails and feeble attempts to get closer to their mother's warm side.

Sabah, needless to say, was overwhelmed with love and a strong sense of duty to the little ones. She licked and nuzzled them affectionately, pausing every other moment to sniff the air and reassure herself of their safety. She wanted to stay with them longer, but she was terribly hungry, and knew that if her cubs were going to eat well, hunting would have to come first. She got up reluctantly, and glanced once more at her sleeping cubs who were oblivious to the dangerous world they would have to face.

Sabah could still hardly believe it; if only her mother and siblings could see her now!

She stretched slowly and relaxed her tense muscles. She tilted her head slightly at a noise behind her. The young cheetah mother quickly turned around with every tooth bared, but she only saw the grass waving in the wind behind her. The noise was just a figment of her imagination.

A little on edge, she walked away. She had to hunt before the day escaped her. Later that day, she returned well fed and strengthened. Her cubs were still alive and ravenous. Sabah let them eat, while she nuzzled them, spoke softly to them, and kept a sharp eye out for a predator.

During their feeding, she finally allowed herself enough time to give them their names. There were two boys and one girl. She named her daughter Jamaa, and her sons, Elim and Chima.

Young though she was, Sabah quickly proved to be a very capable mother. Each time she returned from hunting, she fed her cubs, then scouted the area to see if predators had passed. Occasionally, she moved the cubs to a different den when the area began to feel stale to her.

Her cubs would not be weaned for awhile yet, but weeks later they could clumsily follow Sabah when she went hunting, and soon they were beginning to ask her the few questions their little minds could think of. Elim was the oldest, next came Chima, and then Jamaa.

Sabah loved to answer their questions. Jamaa's personality reminded her very much of herself, but perhaps with a little bit more brain. Her male cubs, on the other hand, were not much like their uncles at all. Both were timid and fearful of anything that moved. Elim in particular was very skittish. It was as if he understood how dangerous his world was, which he didn't in the least. Sabah hoped they would grow out of that.

So far, caring for her cubs had been easy compared to some of her own cubhood memories, but one day the harsh African plains quickly reminded her of just how unpredictable their world was.

The cheetah family was lying on a termite mound. Chima and Elim were pouncing on each other's necks, play biting and chirping. Jamaa was standing near her mother's head while Sabah groomed her. After being successfully pounced on twice, Chima fled to his mother for protection from Elim, who pursued him eagerly, happy to show off, when Sabah abruptly sat up with a growl.

Her mother's quick movement sent Jamaa tumbling down the termite mound chirping with surprise. Sabah had spied a male lion headed straight for the termite mound. She had seen male lions up close before, and each time it struck her with fear and awe, except this time. She bounded down the termite mound, her body tense and straight, with her teeth bared. She carried herself with such an aggressive air, the male lion paused to look at her. He was surprised to see a cheetah charging him; he hadn't noticed the cubs.

Sabah hissed and slapped the ground with both front paws, her eyes blazing. Only the intimidating size of the stronger cat kept her from attacking him. The lion regarded her quietly, his mouth slightly open, as it was a hot day, but the sight of his teeth made Sabah frantic. She snarled loudly and made a short quick charge, thrusting her body forward, then slamming her paws down to act as brakes and to display her rage.

It was a blunder for the young cheetah. If she could have seen herself through the eyes of this stronger predator, she would have squirmed at how defenseless and merely vexing she appeared. Nevertheless, her threat was too much for him to ignore, and her desire to protect her cubs had made her approach too closely. He dove at her.

With a high pitched cry, she leaped out of his reach, only to collide head first into a small tree near a dense wooded area. She jumped up, but the lion was upon her. She turned to defend herself in a fight that she knew would be the end of her, when a crash and deafening roar nearly stopped her heart. A lioness had sprung out of the wooded area and plowed straight into the male lion. The lion was forced to give up ground as the crazed lioness tore at his mane, roaring ferociously.

Sabah was up and away, sprinting

towards the termite mound as fast as her legs could carry her, so frightened her thoughts were blank. Her cubs were not on the termite mound, and she couldn't call them over the ear splitting roars and yowls from the lions behind her.

Overwhelmed, she ran away from the battling lions feeling shocked to be alive. As the noise dimmed behind her, she suddenly realized what had happened. She and the male lion had clearly intruded upon the den site of the lioness, for why else would she be alone, or be so quick to attack a male lion that she most likely knew? Regardless of the reason why, Sabah was just glad to be alive, but now she was a cheetah without cubs, and she needed to find them before the sun set

She glanced behind her. The lioness had driven the male away. Her ferocity was clearly too much for him to oppose during the warm hours of the day. The male lion had turned his face towards Sabah, and she could see his face streaked with red. That was enough for her, and she bolted from the scene, calling for the cubs.

Hours later, the first cub she found was Jamaa, who was huddled in the grass shaking, and unharmed. Next, she found Elim, who was hidden in a manner similar to his sister, but Chima seemed to have vanished. Sabah swallowed hard as she stood over her two cubs. How quickly everything had changed within seconds. She was just about to lead her cubs away, when a shrill chirp made her jump around. Dragging himself out of the grass, Chima appeared, also very much shaken, but healthy. Sabah was overjoyed they hadn't wandered too far after all.

It was not the first time Sabah had had narrow escapes, especially from lions, but for the first time, she found herself seeing all of the danger through the eyes of a mother, which was different. The bond she had shared with her siblings paled in comparison to the one with her cubs, and she suddenly realized she had significantly less control over the survival of her cubs than she thought. Her world was simply too unpredictable for that. She realized the allusion of complete control was just as much to be feared as those raging lions behind her, because it paved the way for carelessness, which was responsible for the death of many.

Sabah herded the cubs to a spot of her choice that had a calming air, and there they stayed, huddled together, each cheetah enjoying each other's comfort and warm reassuring presence.

CHAPTER FOUR

GROWING

After that, Sabah grew more serious. Gone were the days of thinking she had something to prove herself; life was just too busy. There was always one more hunt, or a predator that needed to be driven away, or a cub that needed to be taught a lesson.

Like all cheetah cubs, Elim, Chima, and Jamaa grew alarmingly fast from the perspective of their mother, though it was a relief to see them do so. Sabah quickly tasted the anxiety her mother must have had while rearing her, back when she was reckless. Her cubs were proving to be boisterous and full of personality.

She could tell them apart easily. Each cub had a unique spot pattern that was easily recognizable.

Elim had two large spots on one side of his face that made him stand out, while Jamaa had more black rings around her tail than her brothers, and Chima's face was speckled with many black spots over and around his nose that gave him the appearance of having freckles. Just like her cubs, Sabah had her own particular pattern. She had exceptionally large rings on her tail and many spots around her neck that slightly resembled a necklace.

All the cubs had an appetite for adventure, but Sabah observed that Jamaa did seem to be her most troubling cub. However, she had to acknowledge Jamaa could hardly be called challenging compared to what she herself had put Raisa through during her own cubhood, at least for now.

Jamaa was inquisitive about anything that moved and quick to run after anything that caught her eye. *She is simply exploring and growing,* Sabah would sometimes think to herself, *yet, I can't help but wonder if she also has an unhealthy appetite for the business of the other animals.* Sabah thought this because on multiple occasions she saw Jamaa curiously watching and listening to the conversations of birds in the trees, or the slow thick voiced mutterings of the large hooved animals that occasionally passed them by.

As the cubs grew older, they began to eat meat, which began to change them. Their play fighting grew, along with their strength, and with a sense of purpose behind it, and they looked forward to eating much more than before.

Sabah gave the cubs lessons on how to survive just as how her own mother had given her cubs. "This is very important," Sabah explained carefully. "Just because you are fast, doesn't mean you cannot get caught. When it comes to stronger competitors, fighting should be the very last option. If you get injured and can't run, you can't hunt. You need to know that." The cubs nodded.

"Let me make it more simple for you," Sabah said looking at the cubs searchingly. "For now, just remember this - if you can't run, you can't hunt. Now repeat after me."

"If you can't run, you can't hunt," the cubs chorused.

"Excellent!" Sabah praised, as an overwhelming sense of joy and pride came over her. She was surprised at how fast her little ones could repeat her advice, and she was amused when they would completely forget whatever she had said minutes later. That was to be expected of course.

 CHAPTER FIVE

HYENA CLAN

Now daily life very much reminded Sabah of her cubhood. Surrounded by her cubs, she would gaze across the Serengeti for danger as they played around her, or crawled over her back and gently bit on her tail.

Though prey was plentiful in their area, Sabah began to feel as if it might be best for them to move on. There were not only lions to fight off, but there was a hyena clan that had been steadily growing and had now reached an alarming size. Sabah wasn't exactly sure how big the clan was, but the Serengeti was buzzing about it.

Whenever she led the cubs in search of prey, she could hear murmurings about the clan, usually from the bigger animals she couldn't hunt, but it was the scavengers that knew the most. Any animal that hunted could agree that the scavengers were a nuisance. They attracted the wrong kind of attention at the worst times, and for Sabah, it was usually the jackals.

Jackals disgusted her. They loved to yelp and howl at kills, until they were chased off or managed to sneak in a bite, and their ability to hang around predators at meal times enabled them to learn important information about what was happening between rival predators.

Once, after Sabah had finished a hunt, a jackal appeared on the scene within minutes. The cubs were already on the kill when Sabah saw him, but instead of growling or showing any other sign she was displeased, she called out to him. "What news of the plains scavenger?"

The jackal paused with one paw in the air, and his ears perked. Seeing the cheetah hadn't moved, he inched his way closer. "News?" he cried, his voice shrill for one with such sharp teeth. "There is always news to be told. What would a hunter like you wish to know?" The last sentence was exceptionally polite, since he was eyeing the food as well as the spotted cat. He made sure to keep a respectful distance.

"What news of the hyenas?" Sabah asked carefully keeping her tone neutral and her face blank. When conversing with another animal, it was best not to appear threatening, but she also didn't want to seem friendly.

"The hyenas?" The jackal looked serious, and his tone became more truthful. "They continue to grow. They will flood the land with their numbers soon enough. Their leader is like none I have ever seen; she never rests. She only devours and conquers. Her clan must be stronger than the lions by now."

"I see," Sabah said slowly. She stood over the kill with the smallest hint of a snarl on her face. Now that she had her information, his presence was not welcome. The jackal retreated, and Sabah joined her cubs in feeding.

"Mother," Elim asked, "what's a hyena clan?"

Sabah licked his ear. "Finish eating," she said gently, trying not to sound troubled.

There was just so much to be worried about.

After they had fed, Sabah took the cubs as far away from the kill as possible. Now she wished she had asked the jackal where the hyenas had last been seen so she could put distance between the clan and her cubs, but she sensed she had lost her chance. Her slightly aggressive posture had warned the scavenger she was in a dangerous mood.

"Mother," Jamaa cried trotting alongside her, "please tell us what a hyena clan is. We really want to know."

"Yes, yes!" Chima agreed. "Tell us!"

Sabah turned and regarded her curious cubs who were staring at her hopefully. "I have told you before what a hyena is," Sabah said slowly. "A hyena clan is a group of them, and they are very strong. They hunt together, eat together, and fight together. They are led by a single clan leader, who is very fierce."

"Not like lions?" Elim asked.

"No, not like lions," Sabah answered him.

Lately she had been explaining to the cubs what kind of animals ruled the plains.

Needless to say, she was very particular about lions, since she had lost siblings to them in cubhood and had almost lost her own in turn.

"But can't you fight hyenas Mother?" asked Jamaa with a furrowed brow. The cubs were beginning to notice that Sabah often led predators away from them.

"Well...," Sabah muttered, "not really."

"I will be able to fight them one day," said Jamaa gravely.

"Oh, no you won't!" Sabah nearly shrieked.

Jamaa looked startled, then confused. "You can't fight them," said Sabah severely, "they are too strong for me and definitely for you." Jamaa let out a frustrated little sigh, while her brothers stared at Sabah, also puzzled.

"What about me?" Elim asked.

Sabah jerked her head at him, surprised. Elim was her oldest cub and was still timid. His question seemed out of character, and she looked at him sharply. "No," she answered sternly, "you can't fight them either. In fact, they are stronger than all of us," she added before Chima could ask "what about me?"

The cubs were silent, and Sabah began to feel sorry, though she had no reason to. They needed to be taught they were not invincible. Their instinct taught them to be afraid of larger predators, but it didn't stop their own imagination from trying to reshape their reality. The cubs all looked disappointed until Sabah suddenly laughed at them.

"Goodness me," she chuckled, "you all look like I told you I'd never feed you again." Then she grew serious. "Cheer up," she said, "tomorrow is a very important day, and there is much you need to be thinking about."

"Why?" the cubs asked immediately.

"Wait and see," said Sabah mysteriously.

CHAPTER SIX

THE SCOLDING

The following day, the cubs leaped around their mother chirping with anticipation. Lying on top of a termite mound, her cubs sprawled all over her, Sabah had to slowly sit up and stretch. She yawned and playfully pushed Chima away for trying to chew her tail.

"All right," she said, "now we can begin." She led them through the plains in search of prey. *Today will change how the cubs look at life,* she thought.

After walking for a good bit, Sabah new the cubs were getting tired, and she had decided to let them rest when she spotted what she was looking for - Thompsons gazelles. The cubs hid in the grass while Sabah began to stalk. The Thompsons gazelles, like Sabah, had already had their young, and that was exactly what Sabah was after. A gazelle fawn was precisely what she needed to introduce the cubs to hunting for themselves.

When she had closed the gap needed for a kill, Sabah leaped from the grass and streaked towards the gazelles in long strides. Her long tail wildly swung from side to side, keeping her balanced as she cut through the air.

The cubs could hear Sabah swish through the grass and hoped the hunt would be successful. She was very good at providing for them, but she still missed enough for the cubs to know hunger.

Sabah was flying after a small fawn that was surprisingly fast for its age, and she was almost on top of it, when she suddenly slowed down in an attempt to evade a figure that was rapidly coming her way. She was too late and was struck from the side and almost sent spinning into the dirt by a reckless gazelle. In all her time of hunting, Sabah had never been plowed into by her prey unless it was attacking, and certainly never from a Thompsons gazelle.

She realized as she was struck what had hit her, and using her claws, the cheetah catapulted herself at the reckless animal and caught it by the rump with her paws before subduing it.

As she wrestled with the gazelle, she wondered whether she could still give the cubs a hunting lesson. Even if she weakened the animal enough for the cubs, they could still be injured. *Blast it!* she thought furiously. *Well, I can at least allow them to approach,* she decided with a sigh.

When the gazelle was nearly finished, she chirped for the cubs who came running from the grass eagerly. They paused in surprise, as their food still appeared to be moving. They slowly stepped back while baring their teeth and hissing, but Sabah could tell they were curious. The cubs glanced at Sabah, who only watched to see what they would do. But the cubs still remained wary, the grown gazelle still too much for them.

Sabah decided this would do for now, and she moved in for the kill, when Jamaa suddenly sprang on the gazelle, imitating her mother as best she knew as she how. Elim and Chima joined her, and Sabah watched as they proved that inside, they too were hunters. Sabah finally intervened and finished the gazelle. She praised and nuzzled the cubs affectionately.

"You will all be excellent hunters one day," she beamed, "and do you know how I know?"

"How?" the cubs asked eagerly.

"Because you tackled something bigger and stronger than yourself. It is not every cub that is given a full grown gazelle for their first hunting lesson," Sabah declared proudly. "Now you may eat."

What Sabah said was true. Her cubs were very good at hunting for such a young age. Watching them as they ate, it suddenly dawned on Sabah, that if they survived, one day she would once again hunt with full grown cheetahs by her side.

The days flew by as the cubs continued to receive training about survival. Sitting on a termite mound, Sabah would watch the cubs as they pounced on each other and sprang out of the way to avoid the return tackle. They were also very good natured. Seldom did things get ugly, but when they did, Sabah quickly stepped between the squabbling cubs and scolded them for wasting energy on anger.

Once, a play session between Elim and Chima turned cold, and then hot. Chima was tackled from behind and hit his head in the dirt. He rolled twice from the force and weight behind it. He jumped up, his tail quivering, and nose wrinkled slightly as he let his teeth show. Elim should have respected his obvious annoyance, but instead he jumped on his brother again. They tumbled down the termite mound, Chima yowling furiously.

When it looked as though Chima was going to return the discomfort, Elim leaped away from him and flew to Sabah, who was nodding, allowing herself a bit of sleep from a fitful night. Elim plowed into Sabah, jolting her. Frightened nearly to death by the suddenness of it, Sabah shot straight up nearly five feet in the air, and came back down furious.

"What's gotten into the two of you?" she

snapped. "You're wasting energy on anger!"

"But Elim-," Chima began, but Sabah cut him short.

"Both of you sit down and keep quiet!" she cried.

She looked around, ready to scold Jamaa too, but didn't see the cub. "Where's Jamaa?" she asked Chima and Elim sharply.

They shrugged, and glared at each other. Sabah let out a shrill commanding chirp, but didn't receive a reply. She climbed up the termite mound and gazed around her, anxiety growing. "Wait here," she told them, and she sprang down the termite mound and began to trot away calling for Jamaa.

She paused and studied the grass before her. She could just make out a small beaten trail that only a small body could have made. She narrowed her eyes and followed. It went on until the termite mound was nearly out of sight, and Sabah's ears caught the sound of scuffling. She burst out of the grass to a small cleared area of dirt.

The maker of the noise turned and cast a beady eye at her. It reared up tall and spread its wings on either side threateningly, its mouth opened wide in displeasure at being disturbed. There was a small form near the bird lying on its side, nothing more than a flattened wisp of fur, having fallen victim to the bird's cruel talons. It was a secretary bird, a fierce predator in its own right, and a formidable adversary for a cheetah.

Sabah gazed past the bird and at the small flattened body, a growl building in her throat. The secretary bird swayed on its long legs, allowing more light to bleed through the grass, revealing the color of its prey. To Sabah's relief, it was unmistakably a hare. But where was Jamaa? She was about to turn and leave, when she decided to give another small chirp. This time she was answered.

Jamaa leaped from the grass only a few feet away and greeted her mother joyfully. Sabah was horrified her daughter was so close to this predator. She gave a deep growl, and picked up Jamaa who shrank away at the prospect of getting carried. The cheetah disappeared into the grass, leaving the secretary bird to its kill.

After they had returned to the termite mound, Sabah began to scold Jamaa more than any of the cubs had been scolded in their lives. "What were you thinking?" Sabah snarled. "I try to sleep for a minute and your brothers decide to fight and *you* decide you're old enough to go exploring by *yourself?*"

Jamaa cowered, with her head on her paws. "I heard the rabbit and followed it," she whimpered. "The bird came out of nowhere and attacked it. Mother I had never seen anything like it, so, I…I stayed and watched."

The silence seemed to last years. When Sabah spoke, her voice was cold and stern. "And you didn't stop to think what would happen if the bird had seen you?"

"No", Jamaa whispered.

"Well," said Sabah, "did you see what happened to that hare?"

Jamaa nodded. Elim and Chima fidgeted while listening closely.

"You would have *become* that hare," said Sabah in a voice thick with anger, "so why don't you sit on the mound beside me and *think* about that for awhile?" Jamaa obeyed without another word, and the rest of the day passed without any more notable events.

That was as heated as it got when it came to family squabbles. For the most part, the cheetahs were extremely caring and affectionate. There was still so much to learn, so much to look out for, and breaks between narrowly avoiding death or obstacles of some kind were seldom.

CHAPTER SEVEN

THE BATTLE

One day, the cubs were following Sabah on the hunt as usual, when Sabah spotted gazelles. She told the cubs to stay put. She then glided forward, her body melting into the grass until she disappeared. The cubs huddled together and waited.

"Is she done yet?" Elim loudly whispered hardly ten seconds after Sabah had disappeared.

Chima shook her head. "I don't think so. Let's wait longer."

The three cubs remained still until their ears twitched at the sound of struggling, then Sabah's chirp encouraged them to come out to the feast. They bounded from the grass eagerly, Jamaa leading the way.

The sight of her little ones running towards her warmed Sabah's heart. It was necessary for Sabah to begin the feast. Since the cubs teeth were so small, they could hardly get a bite until their mother's adult teeth had exposed the meat. Once Sabah had gotten her breath back, she opened the meat for the cubs and they began to eat with enthusiasm.

But they were not destined to eat in peace for long, as vultures circled overhead. Sabah found herself feeling uncomfortable and began to squirm. Aside from the vultures, they were still alone, but Sabah urged the cubs to hurry. Elim, Jamaa, and Chima, however, couldn't really eat any faster, and Sabah grew more restless, as a strange feeling came over her.

The Serengeti was quiet, yet Sabah knew an event on a large scale was taking place somewhere, and she desired to know where and what it was. The cubs were still eating, and when a vulture came waddling in to sneak a bite, Sabah pounced, causing the birds to scatter. She pinned the bird down with her paws, her teeth close to his neck. The vulture squawked and thrashed his wings, sending feathers everywhere.

Sabah paid his flapping no mind and moved her teeth even closer to his neck, until he gave up and lay motionless.

"You!" she snarled, "fly up and tell me what you can see from up there on these lands, and I will allow you to have the first share of my kill when you return."

Despite nearly giving the bird a heart attack, the promise of first pickings from rich food was sufficient compensation for the scare, and as a vulture, he was aware that if he approached too close to a feeding, getting pounced on was a risk. He was actually quite fortunate he had been pounced on with the promise of food.

Sabah released him, and the bird eagerly spread his wings and took to the skies. He didn't need to be suspicious of Sabah's intentions. If she had been lying, she would have killed him on the spot, so he had nothing to lose.

Sabah watched him grow smaller, then growled warningly at the other vultures, who were keeping their distance. There were too few of them to push her off the kill, and she had proved she was deadly. Sabah, of course, didn't really care to keep her promise to the vulture, but she was cunning. For it was true that the vultures were in no way entitled to her kill, but showing favor to one could be helpful in the future. There were no true allies on the plains, and a vulture was not company to be desired, but she had heard a thing or two from the scavenger's before.

The vulture returned quickly, but by that time Sabah didn't need his bird's eye view. She could now hear what she had feared. In the distance, she heard the deep thundering of lions and wild screams from hyenas. It was quite obvious what was happening. The lion pride and hyenas had found each other, and a battle had ensued.

The vulture reported eagerly, and Sabah allowed him to come to the kill first, but it didn't hold back the other vultures for long. Still, she had kept her promise.

The sounds of the battle grew louder and louder, echoing strangely, so that Sabah found it hard to pin point the direction of the fight. A lion's roar carries far, so it was very easy to overestimate and underestimate the distance between roars. Sabah then noticed something rising into the air; It was a faint dust cloud. She knew that was where the battle was taking place. It was much closer than she had realized.

She called the cubs to her side, and would have led them away, when a large tawny shape rose out of the grass before her. Sabah nearly yowled. An old, gaunt, and bloody lioness dragged herself slowly towards the cheetah family. The cubs chirped in fright, and Sabah positioned herself in front of them growling savagely, but the lioness wasn't after the cheetahs; she only wanted their kill. She was limping and looked exhausted. The battle had been one of the worst ever seen during her life, and she had been forced to flee.

The sounds of the fighting were growing louder, as the battle drew nearer. The cubs made a run for it, and Sabah, with bared teeth and a lowered head kept an eye on the lion which had sat down and refused to move. Sabah slowly backed away from her, snarling softly. The lioness stood up, and with what little strength she had, charged

Sabah, who promptly retreated. The lioness then made her way to the kill, or what remained of it, and tore into the last few scraps. The vultures hastily hopped out of her way.

Sabah looked around and realized her cubs were, once again, lost. She stood for a moment that seemed like hours to her, furious with the larger cat that was currently eating her prey. She was still trying to process the situation, when the battle suddenly came into view.

Almost an entire pride of lions was in full flight and headed straight towards her and the lioness. The hyenas had completely overwhelmed the lions with their ferocity and numbers.

The sound of the hyena's wild cackling and shrieks nearly drowned out the lion's furious roars and growls.

The lioness raised her head and snarled helplessly. Sabah thought quickly and leaped to the side to avoid being caught in the thick of the fray, as a wave of lions swept by her and were overtaken by the hyena army who were consumed by aggression and victory.

The noise grew deafening as each lion tore or pinned down an isolated hyena only to be surrounded and attacked from all sides by the rest of the clan. One hyena, with a gaping mouth full of teeth, her tail fluffed, and nose quivering, spied the cheetah cowering in the grass looking for a way to escape without being noticed.

Sabah saw a path out of the fighting. In the same moment, the blood crazed hyena lunged at her, but the cheetah's superior speed carried her to safety as the chaos swept the hyena back into the battle.

Agile and swift as always, Sabah evaded any lion or hyena that leaped for her until she had completely cleared the battle ground. Only then did she wonder whether her cubs had survived.

CHAPTER EIGHT
LOST CUBS

The young cheetah mother began chirping for them as she distanced herself from the danger. Never had she been so frustrated. It seemed that as she was rearing her cub's, the world was throwing everything it had at her. As the noise of the fighting dimmed, Elim appeared, seemingly out of nowhere and ran to Sabah's side. Relieved, Sabah gently pushed him with her nose and nuzzled him. Together, mother and cub, they continued their search.

Hours passed; the sun was beginning to set, and still Sabah and Elim searched. Sabah was nearly frantic. If she lost daylight before she found Jamaa and Chima, she would be forced to find a safe place for the night. She couldn't risk Elim being exposed. Sabah decided to change plans.

She left Elim in a sheltered place, and decided to look for the rest of the cubs by herself. In desperation, she decided to take a great risk. She turned and headed back in the direction of the battle. Perhaps, the cubs hadn't made it as far as she had and were hidden in the grass and in danger.

She was making good time at a fast trot, when she spied a small cub wandering through the grass. She bounded towards it, and as she neared, she hastily came to a stop as the cub opened its mouth and yowled. It was unmistakably the rasp of a lion cub. Dismayed and flustered, she stared at it, briefly wondering if it had eaten her other cubs, before realizing it was too small for such a thing.

Sabah didn't dare approach the cub for fear a lioness would hear its yowls, but she continued on. Presently, she came upon the battle ground, which was vacant. She shivered as she sniffed about. The sun was getting lower, and she realized she would have to give up her search and return to her surviving cub.

The poor cheetah quivered, but she wasn't cold. She was angry. Her eyes held a fire as she stood over the battle field, ears plastered to her head, her fangs slightly visible in the dim lighting. It was a good thing there were no scavengers around. Sabah was so heated she likely would have chased down any scavenger that showed its face. There was a squeak behind her, and Sabah jumped around. Covered in dirt, and with one paw in the air, Jamaa regarded her mother anxiously.

"*Jamaa!*" Sabah gasped.

It was nothing short of a miracle and Sabah looked around for Chima too, but it was too late. She had to return to Elim and get Jamaa to safety. Sabah was grateful she was still left with two cubs, but she held a bitter rage against the hyena clan that had caused this mess. Sabah took Jamaa, and soon the two cubs were reunited. The sun set; they were now a family of three.

Sabah wasn't the only cat that had suffered a loss that night. The next day, she learned from a jackal that the lion pride had lost an old lioness and cubs to the ravenous hyenas. The mother cheetah only knew one thing; it was time to get her cubs as far away from lions and hyenas as quickly as possible.

Elim and Jamaa were at first confused and dismayed by Chima's disappearance, but they quickly grasped what had happened and quietly moved on. Cheetah cubs not surviving to adulthood was so common that it had created a sense of knowing that all cheetah cubs are born with. It is that sense that helped them to move on when they lost a playmate. The same went for their mother, however, she had little time to mourn.

Mother and cubs set out on a journey to find an area plentiful with prey and fewer predators. Unfortunately, the odds of finding the ideal area were rather slim. After roaming carefully for a few days, Sabah at last found a place she thought suitable for cubs, though of course only time would tell.

CHAPTER NINE

NEW ADVENTURES

Their new surroundings consisted of open spaces for running and very little dense woodland in range. When she found higher ground, Sabah could see gazelles and other antelope grazing. She was very encouraged, and she wasted no time in securing more meat for her weary cubs.

The next few months proved that her judgment had been sound. While their new territory wasn't completely free of danger, there were very few hyenas and a very small pride of lions that mostly kept to themselves. Of course, the usual animals the cheetahs were quite used to were also in their new territory. At least, that *Sabah* was used to.

As she learned the new territory, Sabah would often climb termite mounds, rocks, or even climb a small tree to scout for prey and to find a decent landmark. The cubs would sometimes climb with her or remain below, watching and learning, but often their curiosity got the better of them and they wandered off. They liked to investigate the different animals they saw which didn't appear to be dangerous. Usually Jamaa was at the bottom of any close calls with some of the animals when Sabah's back was turned

One morning, as Sabah balanced in a tree, the cubs grew restless. Jamaa paused to listen and smell for perhaps a small rodent or an insect, when she detected small scuffling and the sounds of small feet pattering away. Something had been watching them from the tall grass. She craned an ear in the direction of the noise and suddenly bolted off.

Elim chirped with alarm. This was certainly not the first time Jamaa had done this, and he guessed it wouldn't be the last. Whenever his sister took off after a noise, he usually stayed behind to alert Sabah. However, this time, driven by hunger and new boldness that had been steadily growing in him, he followed her.

Jamaa trotted at a fast pace and glanced behind at Elim. She looked annoyed, then shrugged and pressed forward. Elim followed bravely for a few moments before loudly whispering, "Um, Jamaa, shouldn't we-"

Jamaa turned around and gave him a look. "Can't you see I'm hunting?" she asked severely.

Elim didn't say anything else, but he pressed his ears flat against his head. The small pattering grew louder, followed by a faint scratching noise. Jamaa crouched, her small shoulders quivering. Elim crouched beside her. Jamaa lifted a paw and gently placed it on the ground like she had seen her mother do. Then, without warning, she sprang into a clump of grass.

Elim heard a squawk, then a yelp. Jamaa came streaking out of the clump of grass. Behind her a fat bird hopped and flapped its wings against the air in a frenzy of wrath. It uttered strange calls between a cluck and a yell, as it ran after the two cheetahs cubs. Elim and Jamaa ran straight back to the tree chirping for help.

Sabah noticed the cubs were missing and jumped from her perch just in time to see Elim and Jamaa flying towards her with a guinea fowl chasing them. She leaped and pounced on the bird, silencing it with quick work of her teeth. She then looked around because guinea fowl typically travelled in groups. When it was clear they were alone, she slowly turned and looked straight at Jamaa, who gulped and smiled feebly.

"It was her idea," said Elim helpfully.

Jamaa lay down and buried her head in her paws. Sabah snarled softly. Her female cub was really beginning to try her patience. "Jamaa," she said trying her best to not show her teeth, "these plains will not keep forgiving you for your foolishness. Keep it up, and you just might get more excitement than you can handle." She turned away without another word.

As time passed, the seasons changed from lush and green, to intervals of intense heat, drought, and then heavy rain. The cubs found themselves going hungry more than usual, as Sabah struggled under the searing pressure from the sun. Running close to sixty miles an hour during the hot days was rather dangerous, but Sabah couldn't know when she would spot prey again, so she pushed herself to her limits.

CHAPTER TEN

CHANGING TIMES

The cubs were now six month old, and much bigger than when they lost Chima. One day Sabah raised her head from her paws and accidently inhaled some dust blowing in the breeze. She sneezed. "The winds are changing you two," she said as her large cubs looked at her lazily between half closed eyelids.

"What do you mean, Mother?" asked Jamaa, and she yawned and also sneezed when she too inhaled a bit of dust.

"You mean it's hot and dry?" Elim remarked. "It's usually always hot and dry. What's so different about it this time?"

"Once it gets *very* hot," Sabah explained, "many prey animals leave because the grass dies. It becomes harder on many animals, not only for a lack of prey, but also water.

This is the hottest day I've seen since you were born. I'm afraid we are in for an extremely dry spell."

"So that's why the wildebeest and zebra have been so active lately," Jamaa said, thinking aloud.

"There's plenty of water here," Elim protested. "It couldn't *all* dry up could it?"

"You can never tell," Sabah sighed. "I've seen large bodies of water suddenly vanish without a trace when it's hot enough, and others linger when it seemed like they would be the first to go. You just can't know until it happens."

"I think I'm feeling thirsty," said Elim, sitting up and looking uncomfortable. "Do we have to talk about this now?"

"Do you want to learn or not?" asked Sabah bluntly.

"I'd just rather not think about it at the moment. Sometimes, it seems there's always something going on with us," sighed Elim.

"There is *always* something going on in this world. It's your job to be prepared," his mother corrected, "and since you seem so confident, what was one of the first lessons I ever gave to you?"

"If you can't run, you can't hunt," Elim said mournfully.

Excitedly, Jamaa leaped to her feet. "Mother," she cried, "I smell something!"

Sabah got up, but the source of her daughter's fascination came into view before it reached nose. Since it was so hot they had taken refuge beneath a few trees, and above them, cradled in the branches, a large leopard lay with one paw dangling in the air, with its chest and belly supported.

The cheetahs backed away in unison, wondering how long the leopard had been there. Then they noticed the leopard seemed to be asleep. The cheetahs quickly left their shade, glancing over their shoulder to see if they were being followed.

The leopard remained where it was, but Sabah saw an eye slowly open. As the larger cat saw them retreating, an amused, satisfied smile gently twitched her long whiskers, and she stretched her claws before closing her eyes again.

Sabah hurried the cubs a safe distance

away. "Well, that was terrifying!" Jamaa exclaimed. "We can't even relax for one minute."

"That's my fault," Sabah sighed. "I should have been paying more attention."

"Why didn't we smell the leopard," Elim wondered.

"Well, the wind didn't blow much," Sabah said thoughtfully, "but this just goes to show you cubs, that when it comes to these plains, you just never know what may happen."

"All we can do is prepare." Jamaa added.

"Exactly," Sabah agreed, "and practice caution, even when it seems you don't need to."

"Mother," Elim asked gravely, "when will we be hunting beside you?"

"You have a bit more growing to do before its time for that, but I will prepare you. Count on it," Sabah promised.

"Now," she said stretching. "the day has cooled down some. I think we should hunt and find shelter. Does that sound good to you two?" The cubs chirped in response and they set off, all of them keeping a low profile just like they had been taught.

That night, Sabah, Elim, and Jamaa slept with full stomachs, and more determination than ever before. The cheetah family was strengthened as they faced more trials from other animals, just as the loss of Chima had made them stronger, even though they all still nursed grief.

Sabah especially, felt more determined. Her way of fighting her world was to raise cubs, and she resolved that no matter the odds, one day, when she had more cubs, *all* of them would see adulthood.

When the sun rose the following day, the cubs stretched and frisked in the cool early morning light, while Sabah stared across the territory. She scanned the area, her tear marks helping her to see into the distance, but there was not a gazelle in sight.

And so it begins, she thought, *the hard times.* She glanced at Elim and Jamaa. They were chasing each other in circles, until Jamaa cunningly tripped Elim with her paw as if he were prey.

He glanced back at her and chirped before he tumbled. Jamaa sprang away to avoid the return pounce from her annoyed sibling, as he trotted after her.

Sabah's eyes followed them fondly. She then sniffed the air briefly and once again surveyed the area. Finally, she chirped to the cubs to follow her.

The heat viciously beat down on the cheetah family as they made their way through the plains, but the cubs made the most of it, and Sabah began to call upon all her knowledge that was passed down from her mother, Raisa, whenever famine and drought struck.

No matter what happens, Sabah thought, *I will see them through to the end. I may not be able to choose their ending, but I will be there.*

ABOUT THE AUTHOR

Hannah, aka The Whimsy Wordsmith, lives in SC with her parents, two brothers, a sister, and Blackie, her rambunctious Labrador Retriever. She is a fan of Shakespearian plays, as well as the works of Jane Austen and Jack London. When she is not writing, she is either reading or drawing.

In addition to writing chapter books, Hannah is also author of Story Starters for the Imagination and Finish the Story Writing Prompt journals. To see all of Hannah's books, please visit her Amazon Author Page by scanning this QR code.

To sign up for Hannah's newsletter to receive a **FREEBIE** and the latest news and updates, scan this code.

FOLLOW HANNAH ON SOCIAL MEDIA

FACEBOOK

INSTAGRAM

BLOG

If you enjoyed this book, I'd be grateful if you would please leave a review on Amazon.
Thanks!

SABAH'S ADVENTURE CONTINUES IN...

HANNAH E. ENGLAND

CHEETAH
RISING
LEGACY

SABAH'S STORY
PART 2

PREVIEW

CHAPTER 1

It had been days since the cheetah family had eaten. Sabah, Elim, and Jamaa were feeling weak from the drain of hunger combined with intense heat.

"This is getting ridiculous," Elim huffed, yawned, and shook the dust from his coat.

"It's time for another water trip," said Sabah wearily. "Then I'll hunt again."

The cheetahs travelled in single file until they arrived at the main source of water for their territory. Sabah knew there would be prey there, but she was too drained and thirsty to hunt just then, which she regretted heavily.

A herd of impala was already there, drinking and backing away from the water one at a time wary of crocodiles. It was so hot, that not only were prey there, but other predators as well. The cheetahs had to be careful, no matter the circumstances. No was one an ally.

A few members of a small lion pride were there also. There were only four lionesses, and two cubs, which also appeared somewhat thin. The cheetahs didn't know if this was the entire pride, or whether the scraggly cubs were the best the lionesses could do.

The lionesses glanced at the cheetahs. Sabah instantly stopped, her posture shrinking. A lion cub darted to the water's edge and lapped up some of the scummy water eagerly. With warning looks at the cheetahs, the lions moved in first.

Many feet away, and on the opposite side of the pool, Sabah sat down with a petulant expression. A small herd of zebras also tramped down to the pool, and then, upon catching sight of the lions and their strong scent, they wheeled, snorted and pounded their hooves into the muddy water and stampeded back up the bank.

Jamaa chuckled. "Those big sillies. Lions can't hunt while drinking water. Everyone knows that. Now they have made the water worse."

"They are very skittish prey, and not very smart," Sabah answered still keeping a close eye on the lions.

"I'm burning up with heat," Elim mumbled. "Can't we drink now?"

"This pool is not very big," Sabah admonished. "If we drink now, even from the opposite bank, the lions would be close enough to catch us if they tried."

Elim looked at the lions carefully. They were taking their sweet time, speaking to each other softly, lapping at intervals, and watching the water closely for crocodiles.

"What if I asked them not to attack us?" he asked timidly.

Sabah stared at Elim strangely, but instead of becoming angry she said simply, "Well, why don't you?"

Conversing with another animal was not exactly a common occurrence, and for predators in particular, exchanging words was extremely rare, usually because there was no point. It was so rare; most of them would live and die never once hearing the voice of another rival. It seemed insane, but Sabah sensed there would be no bloodshed since everyone was too hot and thirsty.

Elim didn't know what to say. Jamaa looked at him expectantly. "If you can't, I will," she said with an adventurous gleam in her eye.

Elim cleared his throat loudly, but was not heard over the noise of the animals. At last he gave an especially loud chirp. The pool became quiet and everyone stared at the cheetah cub hardly believing what they had just heard.

"If you please, lions," he said timidly, "will you allow us to drink across from you without fear of attack?"

Completely stunned by the boldness of the lesser cat, but also by his polite manner of speaking, the lions only stared for a moment. One of the lionesses yawned and stared Elim directly in the eye. Elim hid behind Sabah.

"Bold for one so young," the lionesses replied, with the smallest hint of a smile around her lips. "Be careful cheetah, where that boldness may lead you. And what, are you frightened already?" she asked noticing he was hiding.

"Face her, Elim," Sabah murmured. "You began this, now finish it."

Elim bravely faced the lioness, though he was nearly overcome by her obvious strength and the intimidating power she held in those yellow eyes. "My request," he said humbly, "I do not think was too bold, O strong lioness."

The lioness dipped her head ever so slightly and looked both amused and flattered.

"You may come drink, little cub," she drawled, "but lions do not make promises for anyone. Still, you have pleased me and my sisters, but I warn you against any impudence."

All the animals were watching and holding their breath. Elim looked at Sabah questioningly.

Sabah, her mouth partly open, was staring at the lions with a beating heart. She shook her head. She wouldn't risk it.

Elim addressed the lions. "I thank you for your patience," he said clearly, "but, I will wait my turn." He could hear the prey animals around him whispering and chattering madly, and there were restless stampings all around.

The lioness turned her eyes to Sabah, "You have taught them well cheetah," she said thoroughly charmed. "He knows his limits, which is very good. I have no doubt that will aide him in the future."

Sabah nodded dumbly. The lions finished quenching their thirst and moved on. Only then did the cheetahs venture down to drink. As they made their way to shade, Sabah proceeded to discuss their experience.

"That was very good, Elim," she said gently, "but as your mother, I have to ask, that even if the lions had given their word, would you have believed them?"

Elim sighed, "I suppose not."

"Good," said Sabah, "I was getting worried there."

"Now," she continued, "I suppose you want to know why I encouraged that."

"Yes!" Elim and Jamaa cried.

"First," said Sabah, "it was our surroundings that gave me the most assurance. Everyone was hot and drained and focused on the water. No one had the energy for a full blown attack. Secondly, I wanted you to have the opportunity to hear the words she chose. Notice how she encouraged you to drink, but made no promise for your safety. Do you know why?"

The cubs shook their head.

"It was about power," said Sabah wisely. "They wished to display it in front of us and their prey. As for their true intentions I can't say, but I would like to think that they were pleased with you enough to let you live."

Jamaa looked very thoughtful. "Mother." she asked, "is… is it completely unheard of to be friends with a competitor? Has it really never been done before?"

"Well," said Sabah looking uncomfortable, "I don't want to say it's *never* happened. We all can be such funny creatures, but I can't think of a reason as to why it *should* happen." She looked at Jamaa sharply. "Are you thinking about making friends with lions, Jamaa?"

Jamaa shook her head, "I just wondered since the lioness looked like she thought Elim was funny."

"Oh, trust me, she did," Sabah said chuckling. "She didn't expect a cub to speak up, let alone so respectfully, and of course it's so rare. It probably had never happened to her before."

She looked at her cubs tenderly. "You both have grown so much. As cubs you seemed so frightened of the world, now just look at the two you!"

"Elim was way more terrified of life than I was," said Jamaa.

"That is true," said Sabah with a smile, "but you both have chosen to control fear and curiosity at such a young age. My siblings and I had a serious problem with that. Now," she said changing the subject, "I think we are all hungry, so it's time to rest up, and then we'll see about a hunt."

The cheetahs put as much distance between themselves and the lions as they could and made their way to some most welcome shade underneath a slender bare looking tree.

CHAPTER 2

Once Sabah was rested, she got up and led the cubs away in search of prey. Trotting along, the cheetahs panted heavily. The scattered grass around them had a slight crunch when they stepped on it, as if it had been baked by the sun, which in a manner of speaking, it had. Dust swirled around them, and heat waves in the distance gave the air a peculiar look.

Elim was nearly reeling. Sabah and Jamaa paused to look at him anxiously.

"Do you need us to stop for you, Elim?" asked Sabah with concern. "We can wait a bit longer."

Elim firmly shook his head. "No," he rasped, "I just want to eat."

Hoping it was just his hunger and not the heat, Sabah continued their search. She wasn't sure how many days they had gone without food. Hunger sometimes made her lose track of time, but even Jamaa appeared to almost have a limp, at least there was something wrong with her walk for sure.

Sabah set her jaw, her teeth pressing tightly against each other. If there was one thing she would defeat, it was hunger. All they needed to do was follow the prey. She lowered her head and quickened her pace.

Though the cheetahs searched and used termite mounds to scan their area, there was not an antelope in sight. As the light dwindled, Sabah had to accept that once again they would sleep with empty stomachs.

The next day brought hope. The cheetah's sleep had been fitful and their muscles felt sore, as they had been tense most of the night. In the darkness they had heard lions and hyenas battling for food; their shrieks and yowls of rage caused Sabah and the cubs to awaken many times to make sure they were still safe. But the light of day drove those fearful noises from their memory for the time being. Now it was time to fill their stomachs.

Sabah stretched and led the cubs through the stricken grass, avoiding bumps in the ground or any other obstacle that would make the cubs use up their strength.

The wind brought Sabah the unmistakable scent of a hoofed animal. The cheetah mother quickened her pace eagerly, even though as she tasted the scent more doubt began to nibble at the edge of her mind. Nonetheless, she followed it.

The cubs kept pace with her while gasping for breath, their empty stomachs clamoring. The source of the scent soon came into view. The cheetahs crouched and remained further away to not attract attention.

The prey was a large male warthog. He walked and nosed about in the grass with a confident gait. His tusks were covered with dirt; they gleamed dangerously.

Sabah gazed at his hide wistfully. To say he would satisfy their hunger was an understatement. She was hungry enough to try, but those tusks made her consider the risks. She glanced behind her at the cubs who had their eyes fixed on her hopefully, their little ears pricked and alert.

Unfortunately, another glance at the warthog made her realize hunting him was out of the question; she was too weak. He would sense her vulnerability and turn on her. She almost growled in frustration, when more rustling and movement caught her eye.

It was another warthog, a younger one, and significantly smaller. Perhaps she stood a chance after all. The cubs saw she meant to hunt and quickly melted away into the grass.

Sabah carefully placed one paw, then another. The warthogs showed no sign of sensing her presence, so she continued. Her body gently moved through the grass with scarcely a sound. The warthogs trotted clumsily, pawing the dirt with their hooves.

Sabah crept up behind them. If they had turned around, they would have seen her slightly raise her head to get a good look at them, revealing her small ears and dark eyes. Without warning, she sprang from hiding and bounded towards them!

The two warthogs sprinted away, kicking up dirt behind them and uttering ear piercing squeals. The bigger warthog, sensing the spotted cat gaining ground, half way turned in his stride and swiped at her with his tusks. Sabah twisted, dashing by him, so that he spun in a circle, and took off in the other direction.

The younger warthog didn't have such good perception, or experience. He only kept running, his little legs moving faster than Sabah could have thought possible. Both of them were a blur as they turned in a circle together and shot by the cubs hiding spot.

Sabah at last, pulled up almost beside the warthog and slapped him off balance with a paw. The warthog stumbled, but not without getting a swipe at her with his tusks. Too hungry to care, Sabah sprang upon him, driven now by hunger more than caution. Jamaa and Elim raised their heads from the grass and chirped encouragement to her. It was done.

Sabah was too tired to eat, but called the cubs, who came and tore into the meat promptly. She sank down, fatigue overwhelming her. It was then she noticed a thin line of red on her front leg. Inwardly she shrugged. First she needed to cool down and eat. She would worry about injuries later.

For a few minutes there was nothing but the sound of the cub's heavy breathing as they ate when Sabah heard Elim snarl. A jackal stood a respectful distance away, ears pointed forward. Sabah managed a surprisingly deep growl, and the jackal stepped back nervously.

The cubs began to eat faster. The jackal took a good look at the cheetahs, and then began to trot around them barking. Sabah could have run him down and shaken him with rage, but the cunning jackal could see none of the cheetahs were in any condition for a chase out of spite.

Jamaa growled between tightly closed jaws. She stood tall, baring her teeth in contempt. The jackal retreated as Jamaa advanced, still growling. Sabah weakly made her way towards the kill and began to bolt down her food, realizing her daughter was buying time so she could eat her fill. Sabah felt strength return as she ate, and Jamaa also came back, though the jackal still followed her barking loudly.

All at once, Sabah leaped to her feet snarling loudly, but not at the jackal who began to retreat. A hyena came swaggering towards them. The cubs got up without complaint and left the kill. Sabah slapped the ground with her paws, her cut sending stings through her leg.

The hyena laughed, and lumbered towards her. Sabah snarled again, but scrambled away as the hyena lunged by her and dragged away the rest of the kill. The cheetahs were left with nothing, but Sabah was relieved. They had full stomachs, and no one was hurt, at least, not *seriously* hurt.

Sabah inspected her injury. It was a clean cut and didn't bleed much, but it stung whenever she put weight on it which worried her. She vaguely wondered whether it had been worth the risk, then dismissed the thought. Of course it had been worth it, they had meat in their bellies didn't they?

Jamaa looked at her mother anxiously, and Sabah nuzzled her, hiding her expression. Elim yawned, looking sleepy, and Jamaa did the same. Sabah laughed at them, pleased at seeing them drowsy from full stomachs. The cheetahs then wandered in search of shade until it was time to hunt again.

Printed in Great Britain
by Amazon

40758021R00056